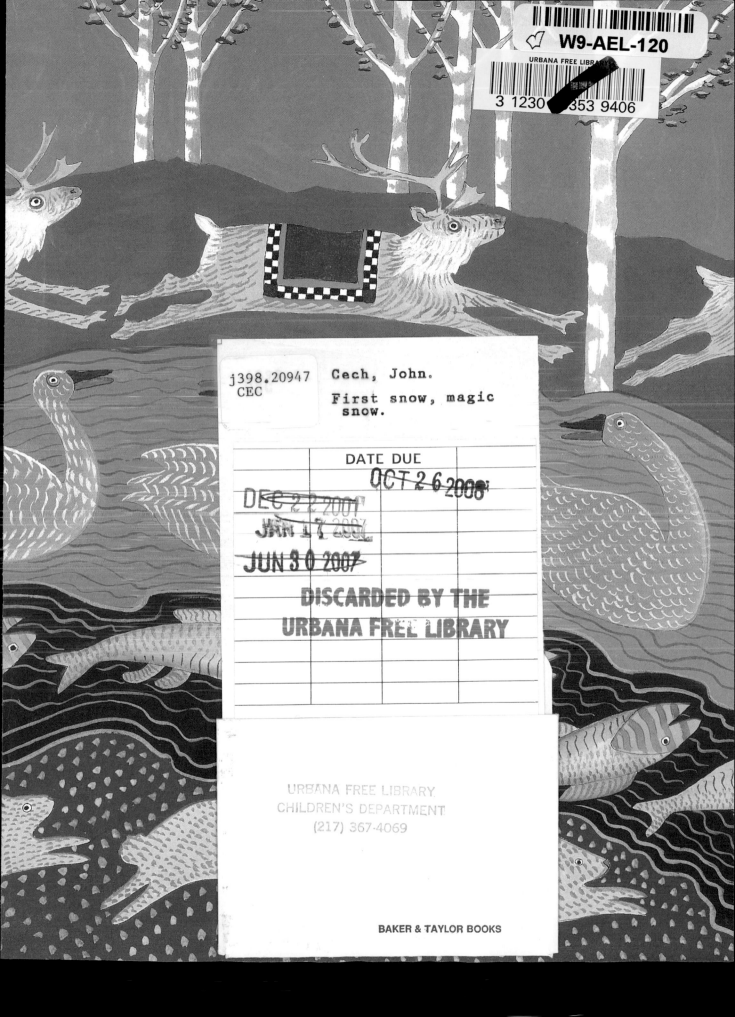

Four Winds Press ⋙ New York

Maxwell Macmillan Canada Toronto
Maxwell Macmillan International
New York Oxford Singapore Sydney

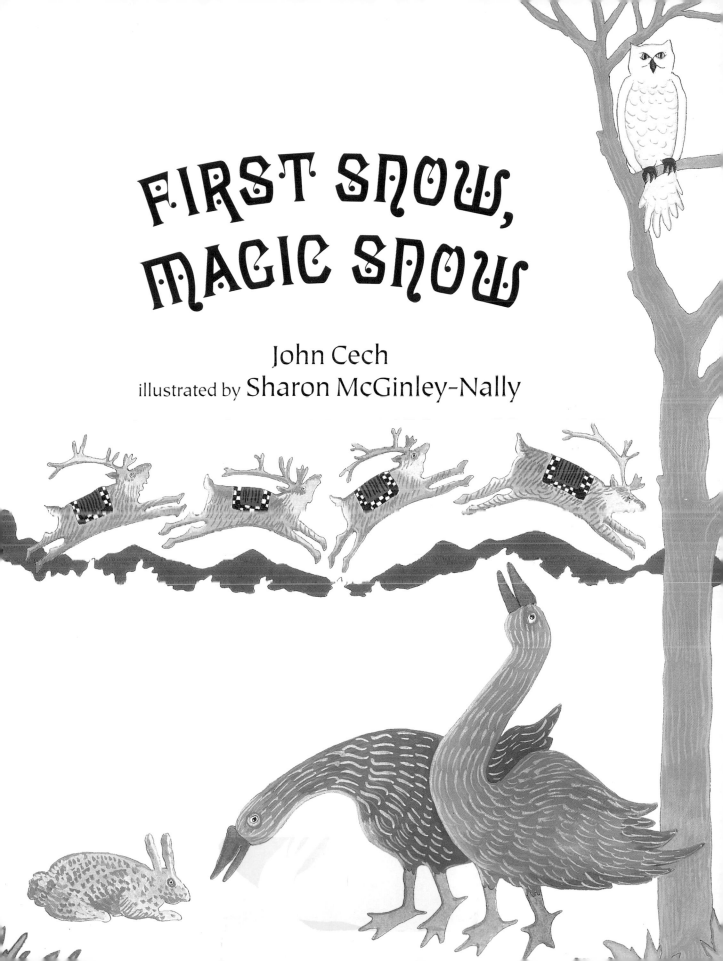

FIRST SNOW, MAGIC SNOW

John Cech
illustrated by Sharon McGinley-Nally

This story takes its inspiration from the traditional Russian tale *"Snegoorochka,"* or *The Snow Maiden*.

The illustrations in this book were primarily painted with Rotring Artists Colors (a liquid watercolor that produces very vivid colors), inks, watercolors, and acrylics. The paintings were color-separated using four-color process.

Text copyright © 1992 by John Cech   Illustrations © 1992 by Sharon McGinley-Nally   All rights reserved. No part of this book may be reproduced or transmitted in any form or by any means, electronic or mechanical, including photocopying, recording, or by any information storage and retrieval system, without permission in writing from the Publisher.   Four Winds Press, Macmillan Publishing Company, 866 Third Avenue, New York, NY 10022   Maxwell Macmillan Canada, Inc., 1200 Eglinton Avenue East, Suite 200, Don Mills, Ontario M3C 3N1   Macmillan Publishing Company is part of the Maxwell Communication Group of Companies.   First edition   Printed and bound in the United States of America   10 9 8 7 6 5 4 3 2 1   The text of this book is set in Tiepolo Book   Book design by Christy Hale   Library of Congress Cataloging-in-Publication Data   Cech, John. First snow, magic show / John Cech ; illustrated by Sharon McGinley-Nally. —1st American ed. p.   cm.   Summary: A little girl made from the magical first snow lives with a lonely man and his wife through the winter, and when she disappears in the spring, the couple set out in search of her.   ISBN 0-02-717971-0 [1. Folklore—Soviet Union. 2. Snow—Folklore.] I. McGinley-Nally, Sharon, ill. II. Title. PZ8.1.C29Fi   1992 398.21'0947—dc20   91-42988

At the end of a cold day a woodsman walked home through the forest. Winter was quickly approaching, and he thought of his wife, their warm house, and the hot soup that they would eat together that evening. He began to sing a cheerful song that put a spring in his step.

But he had not sung his song to the end before he hit a sad note.

"Ah, I wish there was a child in our home, too," he said to himself.

The woodsman and his wife lived in a village of good, kind people, with plenty of children. They had a cat and a dog, fourteen geese, and three cows. They had an orchard of apples and plums, and their meadow ran all the way to the edge of the river. But the woodsman and his wife had no child.

As the woodsman trudged on, snow began to fall. Huge flakes tumbled out of the sky like goose down and soon covered his toes.

"First snow, magic snow. That's what they say." He suddenly stopped. "Well, let's see if it really *is* magic."

The woodsman knelt down and began to pull snow together until he had a nice big mound of it. He patted it smoothly, gently. First he shaped a little head, then arms and legs. He made a hat and a coat for his snow child. When he was done, he tucked the snow child into the hollow of his arm and kissed it on the cheek. He was about to tell himself what a foolish man he was when the child kicked its feet and laughed.

"I must be dreaming," the man said. "But dreams don't kick and giggle." So he wrapped the child inside his coat and hurried home.

His wife came into the yard to greet him. "What have you brought? A peck of potatoes? A lost kitten?"

"No, no!" He was catching his breath. "A snow child. I made it from the snow in the forest."

"Be careful, it might melt inside," she teased him. Then she peeked into the folds of his coat and found a child with berry-red cheeks and the darkest eyes staring up at her. Then all three of them laughed together, a laugh that had tears in it, too.

"We'll call you Snowflake," said the woodsman's wife.

It snowed for the next seven days. Big, soft flakes piled up against the house until the drifts touched the eaves. And while it snowed the little child grew. She quickly learned to balance on her feet, then to walk, and run. Soon she was talking, and one day she made up this song:

First snow, magic snow
Warm inside the drifts I grow
Berry-red, creamy white
Growing through the winter night

Snowflakes fall, snowflakes fly
Little pieces of the sky.

Catch them quick,
Catch them fast,
Or else they're gone,
They just won't last.

By the time the snow had stopped, Snowflake had grown enough to dance, spinning on the soles of the new red boots that her father had sewn and her mother had filled with wool as soft as a whisper. And when the sun sent its bright shafts of light into the house again, Snowflake was ready to step into the white world outside.

Snowflake's heart soared at the sight. Smooth drifts of snow swept down the long hill from the village, and on to the river.

"Who are you?" asked a voice beside her. It belonged to a dark-haired boy.

"My name is Snowflake. What is yours?"

"I'm Vanya, the best sledder on the hill," the boy proclaimed. "Climb on," he said, pointing to his sled. "I'll show you!"

What Snowflake said next got lost in the *quish* of the wind as they sped down the hill. Vanya steered them right up to the river's edge, and then, before the sled shot out over the ice, he made a sharp turn that sent them spinning off the sled and into the powder. They looked like two popovers rolled in sugar.

As they dusted themselves off, a sled came sailing past them and capsized, spilling two girls into a deep drift.

Then another sled, and another, landed in a tumble of legs and arms and shouts and snow until all the village children were mixed together in a pile at the bottom of the hill, along with Vanya's dog, Misha, who slid down on his paws. Misha looked like a white bear, and he never tired of pulling sled after sled back up the long slope as it grew dark and the windows of the houses began to glow and parents called their children to come home for supper.

Soon Snowflake knew everyone in the village, and everyone quickly forgot that she was made of snow and magic. They would have told you, had you asked, that she had always lived in the village, and that they had always heard her lovely songs rising high in the clear, cold air.

Do you remember how winter starts to end? It takes just one drop of water ready to fall from the longest icicle that hangs from the roof of your house. Through the little window of her room, Snowflake watched as that first drop, and then others, steadily grew and fell. The next day she heard a boom, like someone was using the earth as a bass drum. She asked her mother about the sound.

"Oh," her mother said, "it's just the ice complaining on the river before it starts to melt."

"It's not *all* going to melt, is it?" Snowflake asked, as a strange sadness grew inside her.

"Don't worry," her mother comforted, "there's still plenty of sledding left before the butterflies are back again."

But that year the snow left quickly. It grew loose around the trunks of the trees like socks that are too big and fall around your ankles and down into your shoes.

"Come on, Snowflake," Vanya called from the yard one morning. "It's the last day of sledding."

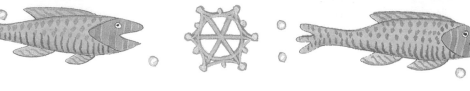

Snowflake watched as Vanya glided down the hill one final time before they would have to go home. She watched him as he let the sled run past her and out across the river to see if he could reach the other side. Then, without warning, he vanished into a black hole that suddenly opened in the middle of the river.

Vanya groped for solid ice, but the edge kept breaking away as he struggled to keep himself afloat. In seconds Snowflake was on the ice, and reaching for his hand. She grabbed it before he went under again. Then the ice shattered, and she fell in, too.

"Hang on to me, Vanya!" she cried as they both floundered in the dark water.

She had gotten one arm around his back and held him. She reached up with the other, searching for a place that would carry their weight. The hole grew wider as she fought the weak ice, which broke and broke again, leaving her treading water. She felt them growing heavier every second. At last she caught a solid edge of ice that held, and she flung an arm over it.

Then she heard Misha's panting next to her, and with her last bit of strength she reached up and locked her fingers in Misha's shaggy coat.

"Pull, Misha, pull!" she whispered.

Heavy as they were, the dog tugged them both out of the hole, across the ice, and to the riverbank. The whole village had reached the edge of the river. They bundled Snowflake and Vanya in blankets and lifted them onto a sleigh. Misha, his white fur steaming, pulled the sleigh up the hill to Snowflake's house.

The villagers watched as the children warmed themselves and drank a special tea made for them by Anastasia Nikolaevna, the oldest person in the village. Vanya's father brushed the boy's hair back from his forehead and said, "It's a wonder you're alive. You must have a guardian angel."

Anastasia Nikolaevna looked at Snowflake and then said to Vanya's father and the others who had crowded into the house, "He surely does."

Soon the only snow that was left lay in the silent, cold corners of the forest. Snowflake hardly ever went out, and her parents worried about her. Vanya and the other children came every day to try to pull her out to play, but she stayed indoors, lost in her own thoughts. Her cheeks no longer glowed, and her eyes lost their brightness.

To celebrate the end of winter, the villagers emptied their mattresses and built a great bonfire with the straw. After the flames died down, the children took turns jumping over the coals, while the adults played music and danced in the warm, green days ahead. To everyone's delight, Snowflake and her parents came to the festival, but she looked pale and weak and sat in the shadows, as far away as she could from the dancing and the singing. Snowflake's friends ran over to her and took her arms, drawing her into their dance around the bright coals of the fire. Then Vanya pulled her by the hand. "Come on, Snowflake, let's jump through together."

"No!" she cried.

"Oh, come on . . . . It's for good luck!" he said as he led her flying over the pile of embers.

But before they reached the other side, Snowflake had vanished. Only a cloud of steam hung over the coals where she had been. Then—with a *pfffftttt!*—it also disappeared.

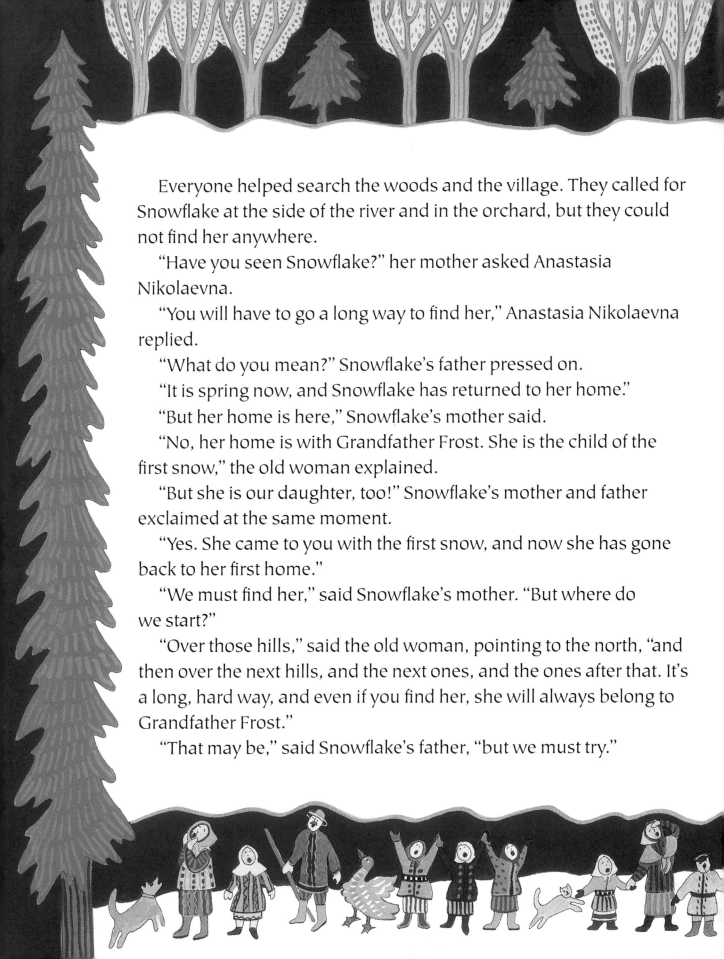

Everyone helped search the woods and the village. They called for Snowflake at the side of the river and in the orchard, but they could not find her anywhere.

"Have you seen Snowflake?" her mother asked Anastasia Nikolaevna.

"You will have to go a long way to find her," Anastasia Nikolaevna replied.

"What do you mean?" Snowflake's father pressed on.

"It is spring now, and Snowflake has returned to her home."

"But her home is here," Snowflake's mother said.

"No, her home is with Grandfather Frost. She is the child of the first snow," the old woman explained.

"But she is our daughter, too!" Snowflake's mother and father exclaimed at the same moment.

"Yes. She came to you with the first snow, and now she has gone back to her first home."

"We must find her," said Snowflake's mother. "But where do we start?"

"Over those hills," said the old woman, pointing to the north, "and then over the next hills, and the next ones, and the ones after that. It's a long, hard way, and even if you find her, she will always belong to Grandfather Frost."

"That may be," said Snowflake's father, "but we must try."

So one fine spring morning, Snowflake's mother and father set off
for the north. The villagers promised to look after their orchards, their
meadow, their cat and dog, fourteen geese, and three cows while they
were gone. With many tears, they said their good-byes.

Snowflake's mother and father walked over hills after hills. They
left towns, farms, and roads far behind, as they slowly made their
way through a land where chilly winds whisper against summer
grasses, where fields of wild tulips stretch to the horizon and
mountains are lost in blue mist. Snow-white hares stopped to look at
the strange visitors before vanishing among the birch trees.
Snowflake's parents walked through brambles and rainstorms, over
sunny days and hard stones, and into cold mornings that kept the
moon in the sky.

Finally, their aching legs carried them to the forest of the Sammi, the people who herd reindeer and live close to the snowy top of the world, where lights play across the evening sky in colored rainbows.

Just before dark Snowflake's parents happened upon a Sammi house. A surprised woman opened the door to the weary couple. She could see they were hungry and cold, so she beckoned them in and sat them down for dinner. After they had eaten, they told her why they had come to the edge of the world.

"So you are seeking Grandfather Frost," the Sammi woman said as she watched the glowing fire. "Ah, then you must go farther north still. I have never seen him myself, but my people say there is only one way to find him: You must reach a place that is open, yet closed; cold, yet warm; quiet, yet full of sounds. There is only one path leading north from my house, and I cannot say if it will take you far enough."

For days Snowflake's mother and father followed that twisting path, until they were tangled in the woods. The branches of the trees closed behind them as they passed. One day, though, they pushed through a group of firs and suddenly found themselves in an opening in the thick forest.

"This is the place," Snowflake's mother said. "I can feel it." So they stopped for the night and ate their last crusts of bread and slept huddled together under the trees.

"Tomorrow," Snowflake's father said, "there will be nothing left of us."

But they passed the night and the next day feeling strangely warm in the clearing, even though the ground was covered with snow.

Then a second day came and went while they listened to a music that filled the woods. But this music did not sound like any other they had ever heard before. It was a soft, steady humming that seemed to come from nowhere and nothing in particular—and yet from everywhere and everything at once.

As the light grew fainter on the third day, they saw a flash of silver among the fir trees.

A tall old man in silver robes walked into the clearing. He had stopped to listen to the singing of the child beside him. He had a face creased with age, and, like the child, he had dark, bright eyes and berry-red cheeks. He nodded and watched the song become a bird that warbled sweetly before disappearing into the forest.

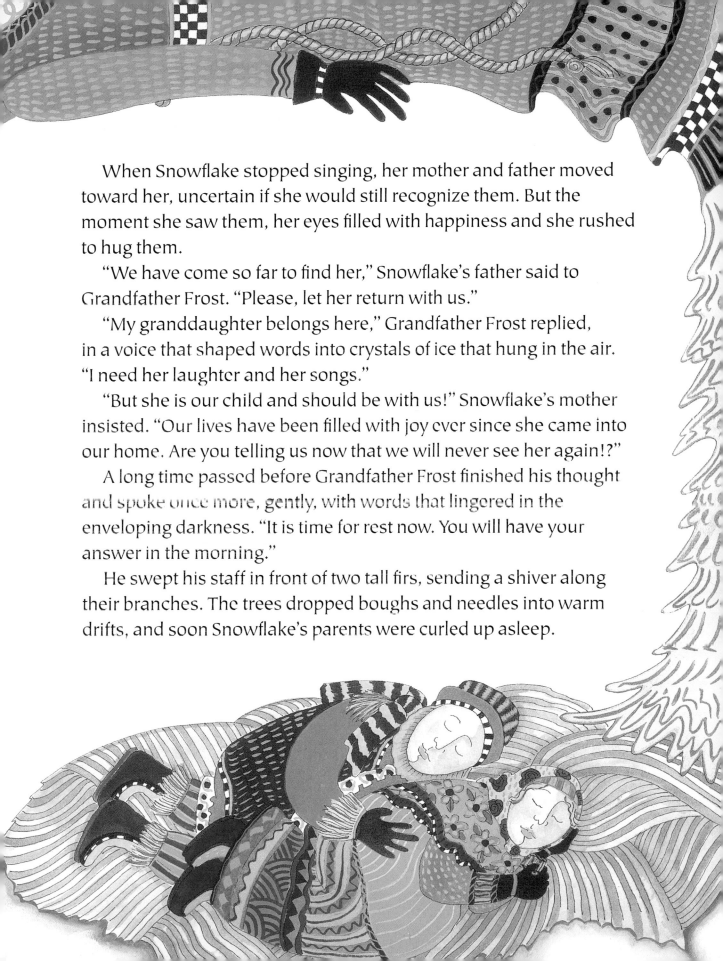

When Snowflake stopped singing, her mother and father moved toward her, uncertain if she would still recognize them. But the moment she saw them, her eyes filled with happiness and she rushed to hug them.

"We have come so far to find her," Snowflake's father said to Grandfather Frost. "Please, let her return with us."

"My granddaughter belongs here," Grandfather Frost replied, in a voice that shaped words into crystals of ice that hung in the air. "I need her laughter and her songs."

"But she is our child and should be with us!" Snowflake's mother insisted. "Our lives have been filled with joy ever since she came into our home. Are you telling us now that we will never see her again!?"

A long time passed before Grandfather Frost finished his thought and spoke once more, gently, with words that lingered in the enveloping darkness. "It is time for rest now. You will have your answer in the morning."

He swept his staff in front of two tall firs, sending a shiver along their branches. The trees dropped boughs and needles into warm drifts, and soon Snowflake's parents were curled up asleep.

They dreamed they were clouds blown by the wind—flying past hills and blue mountains, past birch groves and haystacks. A golden moon hung in the sky as they glided by on their way south.

When they awoke, Snowflake's parents found themselves in a soft bed. Her father looked out the window and saw the bare branches of the plum and apple trees and beyond them the river, and he knew they were home again. A few cold flakes brushed the windowpane. Snowflake's mother looked out the window with him. The fields had been harvested, and snowflakes spun through the yard and around the apple trees.

And then they heard their daughter's song weaving its way from the woods, across the river and through the orchard, growing closer with every word:

First snow, magic snow
With the flurries, home I go.
Snowflakes fall, snowflakes fly,
Little pieces of the sky.

Spring, summer, fall have passed
And now I can return at last—
For friends and joyful company
To parents dear who searched for me
For winter songs and village games
Till springtime sends me north again.